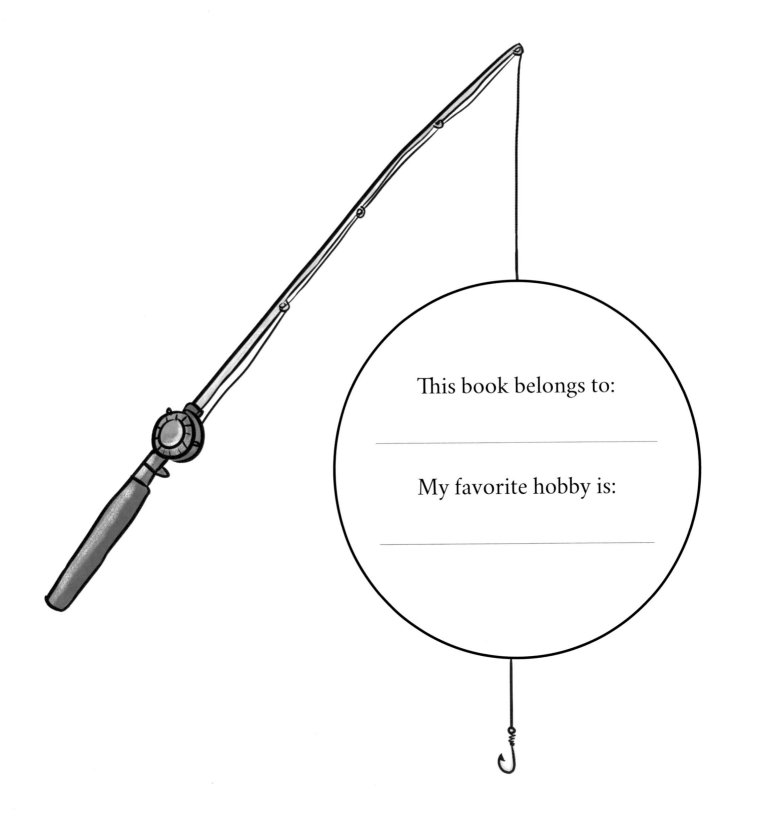

This book belongs to:

_____

My favorite hobby is:

_____

To Hobbyville We Go!

Written by Timothy Taylor & Alicia Santana-Taylor

Illustrated by Robyn Leavens

For Juliana, with love.
–Tim & Alice

For my dearest husband, Sheldon.
–Robyn

Timothy Taylor and Alicia Santana-Taylor
To Hobbyville We Go!

Library of Congress Control Number: 2020921027
Text copyright © 2020 by Timothy Taylor and Alicia Santana-Taylor
Illustrations copyright © 2020 by Robyn Leavens
First Edition

Print ISBN 978-1-7352198-0-6

Book Design | Robyn Leavens
Typeset in Crimson
The illustrations in this book were created digitally
Publishing Support | TSPA The Self Publishing Agency Inc.

Are you bored?
Uninspired?
Big screen TV
on the blink?

Take a look around!

There are
more kinds of fun
than you might think!

The boys and girls of Hobbyville already know

amazing ways

to spend their days!

To Hobbyville we go!

Hobbyville

Aa

Alice sews such
pretty bows.

Bb

Bobby goes to
Broadway shows.

Cc

Camila sings with
all her friends.

Dd

Denise knows all
the fashion trends.

Ee

Ernie bakes his
sweet creations.

Ff

Finn has coins
from fifty nations.

Gg

Gail's an expert
on blue whales.

Hh

Hope has hiked
a hundred trails.

Ii

Irene loves to dance ballet.

Jj

Joel reads comic books all day.

Kk

Katie fishes.

Ll

Larry cooks.

Mary puts old stamps
in books.

Mm

Nn

Nisha learns new
magic tricks.

Oo

Olive studies
politics.

Pp

Paul draws bees
and butterflies.

Qq

Quincy's roses
won a prize!

Raj, Sam and little Tommy
are quite good at origami.

Rr
Ss
Tt

Uu

Uma is a
science tutor.

Vv

Vee writes code
on her computer.

Ww

Willow carves birds
out of wood.

Xx

Xavier's French
is pretty good!

Yy

Yolanda loves
to roller skate.

Zz

Zander's poems
are first rate!

Such exciting things to do,
in Hobbyville and your town too!

So take a day, a week, or two

and find a hobby
just for you!

Timothy Taylor has worked for the Los Angeles Unified School District for two decades as an elementary school teacher, bilingual school psychologist and District administrator. He recently earned his Juris Doctor degree, and plans to establish a law firm which advocates for special-needs students.

Alicia Santana-Taylor is a Licensed Clinical Social Worker with the Los Angeles Unified School District, and a 2019 recipient of the Heroes in Education Award for her inspiring work with at-risk youth. She founded *Alice's Bow Shop* in 2017 after developing an interest in crafting, and hopes that more children will pursue creative and stimulating hobbies.

Timothy and Alicia live in Southern California with their amazing daughter, Juliana, who loves crafting, baseball and ballet.

Robyn Leavens loves to illustrate children's books and lives in New Westminster, British Columbia, with her lovely husband, Sheldon, and two fluffy cats. She loves to draw, laugh, walk about in forests and eat sushi. You can see more of her illustrations at *robynleavens.com*.